MARRIAGE IS A
FLESH KILLER

I0654292

*Our testimony of dying to the flesh God's way,
to represent His kingdom in the earth through
our marriage relationship.*

ELDERS ANDRE & SHARON MOORE

Marriage is a Flesh Killer
Copyright © 2024
Andre and Sharon Moore

CONTENTS

DEDICATION

To my mom, Vera Moore, thank you for birthing me. Through the many struggles in life you encountered, I always had a roof over my head and food to eat. You taught me to be respectful, to not touch anything that didn't belong to me, and to never run from a fight.

She always said, MYOB (mind your own business) and always have car fare to get back home. This may sound minor, but your wisdom kept me out of a lot of trouble. I miss and love you.

Andre

To the late and great Ora Lee Beckam, oh, how I miss you! Thank you for giving me life twice by birthing me and introducing me to Jesus Christ, our Lord and Savior. Thanks for every stripe you gave me for being hardheaded, which was often. The wisdom you shared with me saved my life on several occasions. Momma, you will forever live in my heart.

Sharon

God gave us pastors after his own heart: Reverend Dr. Booker T. Little, Reverend Dr. Richard Nelson, Apostle Daryl O'Neil, and our current pastors, Lonzo and Amia Harris.

Through their teachings, impartations and allowing God to use us for service under their leadership, we are fruits of their labor. We bless and honor them with our whole heart.

To Corine Armstrong, thank you for spending numerous hours teaching me the word and how to pray. In my darkness, you never stopped calling to encourage me; you only saw the best in me. I love you forever!

MARRIAGE IS A
FLESH KILLER

INTRODUCTION

We have been encouraging married couples for over thirty years. As we go through our life process with peaks and valleys, we share our experiences with other couples to strengthen them to stay in their marriages until death does them part.

In May of 2015, we were at a leadership conference where God gave birth to BAMM (Begin Again Marriage Ministry). Since that time, we have been teaching and spreading our insights in churches and marriage conferences across the country.

Psalm 118:17-18 KJV says,

I shall not die, but live, and declare the works of the LORD. The LORD hath chastened me sore: but he hath not given me over unto death.

We believe that no matter what state your marriage is in that God can breathe on it and bring it back to life. But this will only happen if you do it God's way.

In this book we will define **marriage** and **the flesh**. We will discuss how a marital relationship starts in the beginning, how to make a transition to the new, and how to always come back to restoration and reconciliation.

Divorce is not an option is our conclusion.

CHAPTER 1

What is marriage and the flesh?

Let us begin with marriage. Webster's dictionary defines marriage as: the state of being united as spouses in a consensual and contractual relationship recognized by law. As first described in Genesis and later affirmed by Jesus, marriage is a God-ordained covenant relationship between a man and a woman. This lifelong, sexually exclusive relationship often brings children into the world and thus sustains the stewardship of the earth.

The Bible says in Ephesians 5:31-32 (KJV), *"For this cause shall a man leave his father and mother, and shall be joined unto his wife, and they two shall be one flesh."*

Did you know these definitions when you got married? Did you understand what marriage entailed when you said I do? As we write this book, we are going into year forty two of marriage, with a total of forty five years of

3

being together. We had no idea what we were doing when we got married. Love and legal sex were all that was on our minds.

Now that we understand we made a covenant with God and each other, it's not so easy to walk out or hang up the towel or break the vows we made.

Most of us avoid counseling before marriage because we believe it will reveal hidden truths about our mates we would rather not hear. We figure the counselor will talk us out of the decision we made to get married. However, we have it backward: when we get engaged, we should set up counseling before we spend one dime on a reception hall or dress.

What happens in counseling? A number of things, but our process is to ask questions for you as a potential married couple to make a wise decision.

- Why are you getting married?
- Have you accepted Jesus Christ as Lord and Savior?
- What is your credit score?

- Do you have a job and how long have you worked there?
- How many children do you want?

These are basic questions that you should have answers to before beginning a new life together. It will not be perfect; in marriage there are peaks and valleys. However, if you want children and the other does not, it's a problem. If you work and the other does not, are you in agreement? You are making a vital decision that you will spend the rest of your lives together until death do you part; are you ready?

This is where the flesh kicks in. 1 John 2:16 (NKJV), states, *"For all that is in the world, the lust of the flesh, and the lust of the eyes, and the pride of life, is not of the Father, but is of the world."*

What is the flesh? Webster's dictionary defines it as: the soft parts of the body of an animal and especially of a vertebrate, especially the parts composed chiefly of skeletal muscle as distinguished from internal organs, bone, and integument: the condition of having ample fat on the body.

The word **carnal** pertains to the passions and appetites of the flesh. To be carnal is to be un-spiritual, or temporal, to be worldly.

The Bible defines the flesh in Galatians 5:16-21(KJV) as follows:

"This I say then, Walk in the Spirit, and ye shall not fulfil the lust of the flesh.

For the flesh lusteth against the Spirit, and the Spirit against the flesh: and these are contrary the one to the other: so that ye cannot do the things that ye would.

But if ye be led of the Spirit, ye are not under the law.

Now the works of the flesh are manifest, which are these; Adultery, fornication, uncleanness, lasciviousness,

Idolatry, witchcraft, hatred, variance, emulations, wrath, strife, seditions, heresies,

Envyings, murders, drunkenness, revellings, and such like: of the which I tell you before, as I have also told you in time past, that they which do such things shall not inherit the kingdom of God."

The flesh is the part of us that wants what it wants. It hates to be told what to do. It likes to stay in its comfort zone where it's not necessary to change, grow or develop, according to Rick and Denise Renner of Renner Ministries.

The flesh likes excuses: *I don't speak well... Other people are more anointed... I'm not handsome... I'm not pretty... I'm not popular.* Our flesh told us for years why we could not be used by God.

A lot of times we hear people talk about the flesh, but they never identify what it really is. Now that we have God's definition, we can understand and acknowledge when we are walking in our flesh and ask God for help.

We were born selfish; no one taught us that. One of our first words is **mine.** Through our life's journey we become accustomed to doing things a certain way, and now that we are sharing our life with a husband or wife, we find that they don't have the same traditions. In these situations is where compromise kicks in. It's not about selling your soul, nor is it having your way all the time. It's a way of being reconciled to your husband or wife.

As you continue to read this book, we pray God will reveal your personal flesh habits that are preventing you from being that husband or wife God ordained before the foundations of the world.

CHAPTER 2

In the beginning...

Take a journey with us as we explore marital bliss in our newlywed stage. The one thing we wanted was to walk down the aisle to say "I do" in front of God. We did not receive counseling. One of the mothers of the church, Mrs. C, tried to talk to me (Sharon), but I was in love and could not receive wisdom at that time in my life.

My husband had not accepted Jesus Christ as his Lord and Savior, and although I was in a backslidden state, our beliefs were different.

Growing up on the west side of Chicago, he lived on the beginning of the block and I lived in the middle. We always knew each other, but we began dating the summer of 1978. I admired how he would stop traffic and come to the door to get me, open the car door for me while horns were blowing and then take off.

We both enjoyed sports, going to the Bulls games on Tuesday's at the stadium, concerts, walking downtown by navy pier and partying at the clubs. However, our casual habit of getting high extended to trying something different. This lasted years. The new high was marijuana rolled in a joint laced with cocaine, and dipped in PCP, a liquid drug. Back in our time, we called it the happy stick. It was a hallucinating and mind-altering experience. Sometimes people thought they were Superman and they would jump out the window trying to fly. The first hit of the happy stick was our beginning of mind control at the highest level. The devil's drug brought us to a place where it took years to come back from, but God, cleaned us up, and washed away the desire. Even with all the effects PCP could have on you, such as damage to the brain, suicidal tendencies, and depression, God kept us in our right mind, and we do not look like what we been through.

We are sharing our experience with you in hopes that you will not get sidetracked or distracted from the plan and purpose God has for you. Just like the children of Israel wandering in the wilderness for years, the drug had us addicted longer than we wanted to stay.

Her Experience

I could not smoke enough of it. This was our daily routine for seven days a week. The wetter the joint, greater the high. We began to lace the weed with cocaine to extend the high to max, but it still was not enough. The next level was shot guns, using Bic pen tubes. We used five tubes and rubber-banded them together, inserting five happy sticks and blowing into the person's mouth.

This is the reason I praise God so much and very loudly, because we should be dead.

This went on for some years until I started seeing Martians chase me into the house. We tried to stop before, but continued. However, this night was different. I was screaming and running around the house asking my husband to help me, but he was laughing hysterically with tears flowing from his eyes,

I called my brother and sister to come over. While they were enroute, I called Mrs. C. I stayed on the phone with her until my siblings came. This was where my drug habit ended. They begin to call out the demons of mind control, drugs, happy sticks and everything connected to it. I begin to cough and dispel vomit. I released so much that my husband had to get a container.

The process of my new beginning of being free from the happy stick, leaf and cocaine had begun. They told me to fill myself back up with the Word and keep my radio on the gospel station while I was sleeping to maintain my deliverance. This was the day I became a ghost to the drug community and connected to the faith community. The next Sunday, I was reinstated at church and have not looked back.

My husband and I always did everything together, but now there was a void because I no longer desired to get high. The other parts of my flesh were not delivered like my mouth, so I was rough around the edges, especially when my husband provoked me. I needed help in walking this faith walk out because I still loved my husband, but he was still doing what he was doing. God sent me help from the sanctuary by the name of Mrs. C.

She had me reading scriptures and then she would discuss what I understood about my assignment. She showed me how to pray the word for myself and my husband. I loved my husband and wanted him to worship with me. On Sundays I would leave the seat open next to me to imagine him praising God with me.

One day Mrs. C asked me, "How are you representing God in front of your husband?" She quoted 2 Corinthians 5:20 (KJV): *"Now then we are ambassadors for Christ, as though God did beseech you by us: we pray you in Christ's stead, be ye reconciled to God."*

This was when my service to my husband began. I understood the scripture to say that he must read what I do and not what I say.

Everyone thought I was crazy when I was serving him meals, running his bath water, and rolling his weed, and he was not even working at the time. When we went to the grocery store, I would give him the money in the car so he could feel good paying the bill. At this point in our marriage, I could not see my husband with my eyes; I asked God to let me see him from His eyes.

I wanted my husband saved, so I honored him even when he was not worthy. I loved him, even when he did not deserve it and served him with love. Many said I was a fool, but love covers a multitude of sins, so the Bible says. I would pray for him daily out loud so he could hear me: "God, I thank you that ___ is the head and not the tail, he's above and not beneath, he's a lender and not a borrower"; Psalm 1:1-3, "Blessed is the man that walketh not in the counsel of the ungodly, nor standeth in the way of sinners, nor sitteth in the seat of the scornful.

But his delight is in the law of the LORD; and in his law doth he meditate day and night.

And he shall be like a tree planted by the rivers of water, that bringeth forth his fruit in his season; his leaf also shall not wither; and whatsoever he doeth shall prosper."

I prayed this daily and did not take time off because love is an action word; it has movement, it pursues, demonstrates, and makes others shine at your expense.

His Experience

It was just me getting high. My best friend no longer wanted to indulge. I wasn't working, but I was getting high every day. My wife had the gospel radio station on all night. She was going to Sunday school and church, even during the week. This was totally different, but I knew how to make her mad enough to curse me out.

I went to church with her one day and it wasn't all that. Came home to get my happy stick, beer and watch the game. There was a void now because my wife did not hang out like we used to. Our conversations had changed. I loved my wife, but I was not liking her new lifestyle. We needed to return to the way it was before daily church.

There were several times I wanted to give up drugs. I even went as far as flushing them down the toilet, but then I would retract by saying, "What the hell did I do that for?" I would go and buy more. I got to the point of being sick and tired and needed a change.

I begin to ask God to take the desire from me, but still got high every day. Until one day I heard God say, *I have already delivered you.* This was my process. The beginning was to ask even though I didn't see the manifestation. I continued to ask to be free from the desire.

Sharon was gone to church again, and I was sitting by myself getting high and suddenly, everything went completely silent. I thought I was dead. I called my mother and said, "Momma, I love you, I'm dead." My mom and oldest sister had the landlord open the door. There I was, laying on the couch in my underwear, high as a kite. My mother was relieved; she thought I had killed my wife.

The following Sunday, my wife was getting ready for church, and I asked her, "Where are you going?"

She replied, "I'm going to Sunday school; do you want to go to church today? I will come back and get you."

I said, "I am coming with you now," and I have been in church ever since.

I accepted Jesus Christ as my Lord and Savior in December of 1988 and I'm still learning. However, my wife and I serve God together in the same faith community.

My wife loved me past my ugly. She demonstrated her love through what she did, not so much what she said. Yeah, I heard the prayers, but the way she loved me in my mess and still called me King was a feeling that could not be explained.

In order for our marriage to live, we both had to die to the flesh and allow God to live and guide us in His spirit.

These may be some helpful tips in getting to a place of peace and communication with your spouse.

1. Confess your faults often
2. Forgive quickly
3. Avoid the outside noisemakers
4. Remember the vows you made with God and each other

5. Family does not come before your husband or wife

As we move to renew our minds with God's word and direction, we understand that transition is not easy, but necessary.

CHAPTER 3

Transition

Several wounds were opened during our transition process that had to be healed. Now that we were both saved and serving in the house of God, we were beginning to live out this scripture:

2 Corinthians 5:17 (KJV)

Therefore if any man be in Christ, he is a new creature: old things are passed away; behold, all things are become new.

The meaning of transition from Webster's dictionary is the process in which something changes from one state to another. The transition of childhood to adulthood. Between roles, disengagement from one role and engagement in another.

When you are in the process of transitioning, it can only begin when you tell the truth about where you are inwardly and outwardly.

Therefore, we were in the neutral zone, helping one another to begin again.

What happens when you transition?

Why do I want to transition?

How do you know if you have made the transition?

We had a lot of catching up to do as far learning the scriptures, what Jesus did and why.

During this time of transition, God was drawing us to Himself and that began with a love for the Word, prayer and each other. When this happened, friends we used to hang out with did not want any part of our faith in God. Therefore, we left those people behind and moved forward with God. This did not happen overnight, but in the process of pursuing God, our conversation changed along with our desires. We no longer wanted to get high or do those things that had us bound. We hungered and thirsted for the truth of God's word.

Our lifestyle consisted of work, church and home. The calls decreased concerning the parties and DJs. We learned that friends will either come with you or you have to leave them behind.

We must give a shout out to Greater Open Door MB Church for their Sunday School program and all the superintendents for their encouragement and making us accountable to the word of God. One year after he accepted Christ, Andre was teaching the adult class and I taught new members. When you decide to separate yourself and seek the Kingdom of God, all other things shall be added unto you.

There was such a hunger for the Word, and we were grateful for what God had done by bringing us out of the kingdom of darkness into the Kingdom of His dear Son. We held onto this scripture: Romans 8:38-39, *"For I am persuaded that neither death nor life, nor angels, nor principalities, nor powers, nor things present, nor things to come.*

Nor height, nor depth, nor any other created thing shall be able to separate us from the love of God which is in Christ Jesus our Lord."

We are still in process, working on our marital issues that we can't discuss openly right now. We still have heated fellowships, disagreements and some troublesome memories that we are working through as God shows us ourselves in the Word.

One thing we learned was that men think different from women. When men say, "I'm sorry," most of the time they think everything is resolved. However, depending on the comment, it can cut us deeply and they cannot see the internal bleeding or that we have shut down. This is why it's important to communicate from the inside out, so true forgiveness and restoration can come to your marriage.

Although we were working in the church we still had unresolved issues in our marriage. Most of the time we put our game face on as if everything was okay, and we never got help. The Bible says to confess your faults one to another that you may be healed. However, we remained silent because we didn't want anyone to know our business or what was going on in our house. In these cases, most of the time it results in divorce because of a loss of communication and continued separation in intimacy and finances.

However, real change takes place when there is vulnerability on both sides. When we are not afraid to be naked and honest talking with our husbands and wives in love, that's when the breakthrough comes.

The peaks and valleys you share become your personal experience with one another, and the storms that God brings you through increase your trust. Insecurity is no longer a tool the devil can use to discredit one another.

Through pursuing God and studying His Word, you look up one day and realize your behaviors have changed. The word of God has you to look within yourself and not to find fault with others. We found that we had to unlearn old mindsets to understand the mind of Christ.

Romans 12:2 (KJV) states, *"And be not conformed to this world, but be ye transformed by the renewing of your mind that ye may prove what that good and acceptable and perfect will of God".* The problem with most marriages is we want to be like other marriages without understanding they have struggles too. It may look good on the outside, but inside the house there may be several storms going on. If we would conform to the word of God concerning our marriage, then God would give us what we need to dissipate our personal storms.

Sometimes in our marriages we set up barricades because of past relationships we have not dealt with. Therefore, our husbands and wives are only receiving a portion of us because of the fear of reliving past traumas of what someone else did to us in a prior relationship. We must understand, there is always a chance you can be hurt when building a new relationship, whether it's marriage, friendship, or church.

What does marriage look like to you? Is conflict and selflessness a part of your answer? **Marriage is a flesh killer.** The Bible says, "the two shall become one flesh". Part of understanding each other is not always demanding our way but ensuring the other person's needs are met and wanting to serve the other more than having our way. This is how we know our flesh is being crucified.

As we move from transition to restoration, there are three ingredients we should include in our daily walk with our spouses:

1. **Love-** How are you demonstrating love without talking?

2. **Humility-** Do you always have to take the lead? Is chief the only position you want?

3. **Serving-** Jesus was the epitome of serving. In what capacity do you serve?

CHAPTER 4

Restoration

Webster's dictionary defines restoration as follows: to bring back to or put back into a former or original state; renew.

When you have been damaged by your way of thinking, living by incorrect principles, and engaged in darkness of the world, your mind has to be renewed.

We talked at the end of chapter three about love, humility, and serving. Being loved is the most powerful motivation in the world. Our ability to love is shaped by our experience of love. We usually love others as we have been loved.

In Romans 5:8-10 (KJV), it states, *"But God commendeth his love toward us, in that, while we were yet sinners, Christ died for us.*

Much more then, being now justified by his blood, we shall be saved from wrath through him.

For if, when we were enemies, we were reconciled to God by the death of his Son, much more, being reconciled, we shall be saved by his life.

When we learn to walk in humility and servitude with one another, as we grow it's not that easy to get rattled over any little challenge we encounter. Jesus is always the example, and He walked it out even when it meant his death. He washed the disciple's feet, serving in total transparency. Read John 13.

Philippians 4:7-8 (KJV)

But made himself of no reputation, and took upon him the form of a servant, and was made in the likeness of men:

And being found in fashion as a man, he humbled himself, and became obedient unto death, even the death of the cross.

How do you know if your marriage has been restored?

To us, restoration means that we can communicate without bringing up past hurts or unfinished arguments. There is no more holding grudges. I no longer need to see Andre out of God's eyes. When I see him now, I see a man in love with God, my protector, my provider and my best friend. We can walk down the street holding hands, eating ice cream and we don't care who sees or what people say.

We still have heated fellowship, but it does not last for days. We forgive quickly, not allowing the devil a place to set up a wedge between us. It's important for us to maintain our marriage by attending marriage conferences and continuing to invest and educate ourselves in our union.

Are you playing the blame game? Are you blaming other people for where you are in life, and not taking ownership of the decisions you made? We made a choice to work through our marriage God's way and we received God's results with total restoration. We're not as young as we once were, we've gained extra pounds and lost some hair, but we love each other more than before because God blessed us through His word teaching us how to die to our flesh.

I know God restored the relationship because of our freedom to share any and everything with each other. We no longer worry about trigger words that may set one of us off. Through the process of life and both of us desiring for God to be the head of our lives, we can confess our faults one to another, not always agreeing, but respecting each other when we do not agree.

When you no longer have a barricade around your heart for your husband or wife, you believe what he or she says. It does not mean you are foolish, but you made a decision to trust the God in them and not remember what he or she used to do. This is what God does for us daily; He forgives our sins as we forgive those who trespass against us. However, He does not bring it up again.

Most people do not believe total restoration exists, and it's because they are not willing to kill their fleshly mindset. They are not willing die to their ungodly desires. They're consistently set on having their way, they have no desire to compromise, and it's all about them, but they still want to be married.

One thing that has helped our marriage tremendously is attending various marriage conferences. Although we attend conferences from time to time, we consider marriage conferences only for people who are having problems, not as a form of preventive maintenance.

Restoration starts when you as a believer understand and believe you can ask God to change you and make you the best believer you can be. When you submit yourself to God and do what He called you to do, all the other things will be added unto you.

Matthew 6:30-33 (MSG)

"If God gives such attention to the appearance of wildflowers—most of which are never even seen—don't you think he'll attend to you, take pride in you, do his best for you? What I'm trying to do here is to get you to relax, to not be so preoccupied with getting, so you can respond to God's giving. People who don't know God and the way he works fuss over these

things, but you know both God and how he works. Steep your life in God-reality, God-initiative, God-provisions. Don't worry about missing out. You'll find all your everyday human concerns will be met."

One reason we do not restore others is because we wonder about what other people will think or say about our decision. God forbid that we are considered a punk because we choose to save someone who left us for dead, feed someone who left us hungry or house them when they ran off with the rent money. This is the strength of the kingdom when you can live the below scriptures.

Luke 6:33-38 (KJV)

"And if ye do good to them which do good to you, what thank have ye? for sinners also do even the same.

And if ye lend to them of whom ye hope to receive, what thank have ye? for sinners also lend to sinners, to receive as much again.

But love ye your enemies, and do good, and lend, hoping for nothing again; and your reward shall be great, and ye shall be the children of the Highest: for he is kind unto the unthankful and to the evil.

Be ye therefore merciful, as your Father also is merciful.

Judge not, and ye shall not be judged: condemn not, and ye shall not be condemned: forgive, and ye shall be forgiven:

Give, and it shall be given unto you; good measure, pressed down, and shaken together, and running over, shall men give into your bosom. For with the same measure that ye mete withal it shall be measured to you again."

Restoration is not an option; it's what we were born to do. It's the heart of our Lord Jesus Christ. We should desire to be like Him. If you are married and want to have the fullness of the Garden, being naked and not ashamed before you leave this earth, ask the Savior to help guide you to the place of Eden on earth.

What do I mean about Eden? It was the first place of true relationship with God and each other without sin. Notice, wherever sin enters, it separates. When Adam and Eve sinned in the garden, they were separated from

God. Now our journey is to get back to God through our Lord and Savior Jesus Christ, which was God's original intent.

CONCLUSION

Our flesh produces chaos when it does not get what it wants. The most difficult part of marriage is admitting that you have a problem controlling the flesh that is not submitted to God. Everyone is right in their own eyes until we surrender to God and allow Him to show us ourselves.

The problem that ruins most marriages is lack of communication or refusing to discuss what's bothering us in a relationship. Another is unfulfilled sexual desires or not being able to bring our fantasies into our bedrooms. Therefore, we imagine being with or watching that particular thing on screen or in real life. Holding grudges or always bringing up the past arguments that we have forgiven each other for is another barrier. Finally, not putting all finances together. Remember the famous cliché, "Don't let the right hand know what the left hand is doing?" This is another way of hiding money from each other. A lack of goals, plans, and unity brings separation.

When these areas are not under God's care, things happen like bad decisions, lack of interest in going to church, and decreased study and prayer time. They are all distractions that come to prevent us from reaching our purpose. We are not saying that if you follow these steps, you will never have a disagreement. What we are saying is that if you keep God first, you will handle your distractions with a better resolve. The only perfect marriage that ever existed was Adam and Eve; however, deception caused them to sin and it was the first separation from God's plan.

In the beginning we were looking for a high that we could never receive again. All the money spent, lies told, schemes, hurtful words spoken, and deception that we were living a good life were temporary insanity. When you hear the voice of God in the midst of your insanity, it's time to come home. It's time to transition back to God and live.

We know it's not easy, but each person has to make the decision that they are sick and tired of being in a place of death and destruction. We have to choose Roman 10:9-10, to confess our sins and ask God to forgive us. This will help us move to our next step. If we continue to blame people for where we are in life, not accepting the decisions we made, we will miss the opportunity to be restored.

Whenever Israel repented to God, He restored them. However, when they were in a backsliding position, their favor and protection from God left with their disobedience. It's no different for us, being the spiritual Israel. When we disobey God's word, we are no longer operating under the principles of God's kingdom. The decisions we make are under the kingdom of this world, so we receive their results and not God's best for us.

Restoration does not mean that I will be the same size I was when I got married, although my sins have been forgiven. The damage I did while in sin will still be accounted for; however, the restoration is knowing that my mind has been renewed by the word of God. I will not continue in sin. The pain and tragedies we went through, we can hold one another and say God brought us through.

Each of us can choose to love unconditionally like Jesus did for us, our past, present, and future. Restoration is there when loves covers and see no faults. Although we still fall short, make mistakes, and engage in heated fellowship, we are quick to forgive and restore rather than to blame. To me that's restoration; loving me where I am, until God perfects me to where I should be.

We hope that by reading this book, you would find hope in your marriage. Let each of you work on killing your fleshly emotions that prevent marriages from reaching their oneness on earth as it is in heaven.

This is our prayer based on Psalm 1:1-3. Please feel free to pray for your marriage and insert your names:

Blessed are Andre and Sharon, who walketh not in the counsel of the ungodly, nor standeth in the way of sinners, nor sitteth in the seat of the scornful.

But Andre and Sharon's delight is in the law of the Lord, and in His law doth Andre and Sharon meditate day and night.

Andre and Sharon shall be like trees planted by the rivers of water that bringeth forth their fruit in their season: Andre and Sharon's leaves shall not wither, and whatsoever Andre and Sharon doeth shall prosper.

ABOUT THE AUTHORS

Elders Andre and Sharon Moore were born and raised on the west side of Chicago.

Andre received his 48-Hour security training from Triton Junior College, where he obtained employment from Oak Park River Forest High School as a Safety Support Officer for 27 years.

Sharon attended Augustana College, then later graduated from Northeastern University with a BA in Liberal Arts.

Andre and Sharon are the Founders of BAMM (Begin Again Marriage Ministry), which was birthed in May 2015. The purpose of BAMM is to enhance marriages through biblical teaching by understanding God's purpose for marital unions. They help to establish strong marriages which equates to strong families, communities, churches, and citizens.

Andre and Sharon have been teaching and preaching over 20 years, encouraging the body of Christ to stay focused and keep their eyes on God by finishing the course set before them.

God is good and His mercy endures through all generations!

Andre and Sharon can be reached for questions or ministry at the email addresses listed below:

Andre: Mooreandre612@yahoo.com
Sharon: Slmoore0223@yahoo.com